FORECAST / PRONOSTICO

VICTOR VELEZ

Forecast/ Pronóstico
ISBN (softcover): 9781980666431

© 2023 Cover design and photo by Victor Vélez

Copy Editor: Emma Marie Willig
Text Formatting by Document Whisperer LLC
Sub-Title Quote by John Naisbitt

www.anjelissebooks.wixsite.com/anjelissebooks

Printed in the United States of America
Font: Goudy Old Style

For those seeking a purpose in life.

The most reliable way to forecast the future
is to try to understand the present.

John Naisbitt

PROLOGUE

Imagine being everywhere, seeing and feeling everything at will- that's me. I see all life, love, compassion, hate, evil, beauty, and darkness. I see what others do not see. I see things that not even I can explain in my surreal existence. I see a famine of spiritual thirst, humanity's search for purpose and balance. I see the past and present but not the future. I am merely flipping pages of several lives, discovering unexplainable occurrences, mysteries of the human experience that leave us in a state of wonder. Like air, I surround every situation and stand silently in the background. I cannot change any conditions or alter outcomes. Like in all human tales, I've seen happy endings, many sad endings, and massive twists and turns you would never expect. I am simply an observer, telling you another story...let me introduce you to Moisés.

MY NAME IS MOISES. *I lived in "Spanish Harlem" in New York City, better known as "El Barrio," for many years. After my father's death, I left the hustle and bustle of the big city- and moved to the eastern coast of Massachusetts, near Boston, by the seashore. I took my mother and my sister to live with me. I worked at a print shop.*

After some years, I found myself emotionally lost. I was bored of the same routine and saw the world in black and white. Anxiety was a daily friend.

Then life, in its mysterious ways, stood before me and challenged me to see and fulfill my greatest potential. It was at this moment I had to step back and evaluate my life- look in the mirror and confront my inner self.

It all started one Thursday evening 30 years ago. I experienced the most unusual three days of my life.

THURSDAY EVENING

THE FORECAST PREDICTED a thunderstorm. Everyone at the print shop was attentive to the developments. We all experienced many storms in the coastal areas, but this storm was personal.

I lived in the small town of Sea King, off the eastern coast of Boston, with about forty thousand residents. I purchased a small family house by the sea some years ago, loving the sound of ocean waves ending their journey on the shore. Sea King wasn't known as a tourist attraction. The people's livelihood was fishing and fish markets along the shorelines, the best on the Eastern coast.

It was a regular day at work, though all week I worked 'til 9 p.m., that day, I left at my normal time. A couple of co-workers invited me for drinks at the corner tavern at Joe's place. Thursdays were *happy hour* I decided to go. I hadn't been feeling good. Something was eating me up inside- I was feeling anxious and having difficulty sleeping.

Heading to the bathroom, I passed by the window overlooking the town. I noticed dark blue clouds slowly creeping toward the shore in the distant sky. The thunderstorm was on its way, as predicted. I remember seeing a tugboat...it was strange, but I could hear, in my mind, the old grueling engine struggling...heading out into the sea. I thought to myself. *Why is it going toward the storm instead of away? Is someone in trouble?*

"Moisés, are you going to Joe's?"

I turned, "Yeah...yeah, I'll be there." I went on to the bathroom and then headed to the tavern.

The tavern was buzzing as usual. Music, people chatting, eating, and drinking. The guys were already on the side of the bar area. I walked up to Raiden.

"I guess you're canceling your fishing trip tonight...with this storm coming."

"Yeah, bummer...have to reschedule," Raiden said.

"They're talking about a big one coming," Fishstick said. His name is Shant; he loves fishing and is skinny, so we call him *fishstick*.

"Hey, Moisés...you're into movies. You saw the previews of that new dinosaur movie coming out?" Jim yelled out.

"Oh yeah...something *park*."

"Jurassic Park," Alec shouted out.

"Yeah, that one. It looks good," I commented.

"Well, Steven Spielberg, what'd you expect," Jim said. Gail, the bartender, makes her rounds, asking who needs a drink.

After a few more drinks, I heard thunder closing in on the tavern. I got my belongings, said goodbye, and headed to the car.

The rain got stronger, and the wind picked up. The "Sea King Deli" sign swayed back and forth across the street. I started the car and immediately put on the radio to hear the forecast, got only static. I drove as the rain got harder; I tried calling my mother but wasn't getting through. Looking at my rearview mirror, I saw the dark blue clouds overtaking the sky, hovering over this small town. I finally arrived home and parked my car. As I opened the car door and my umbrella, I ran toward the house. I heard the sound of the old engine grueling behind me. I turned and looked out into the shore and saw nothing but fog. I listened carefully. I heard a faint whale calling sound... then it stopped. I looked at the sky; thunder and lightning were above us, like a rage.

I opened the front door and entered my house. I shook the umbrella and put it by my muddy boots.

"Wow! Bad weather out there." The lights in the house started flickering on and off. I put my belongings down and looked for candles; I went to the kitchen drawer and found one white candle. I put it on the table, just in case.

"¿Ma?...Mom!" Then, I noticed the shower was running. She had the radio on. She likes listening to her old-style music. My sister, Sully wasn't home yet from class; she was a junior at "Bridgewater State College." They interrupted the music for a weather forecast. I turned up the volume on the radio:

"A *powerful Northeastern thunderstorm will continue to move over the region for the next few days. This storm will bring heavy rain and dangerous conditions along the coast. A thunderstorm warning is in effect. In other news....*"

I picked up the mail on the kitchen table when I heard that whaling sound again. At first, I thought it was coming from the radio. I lowered the volume...it was coming from outside the house.

"What's that sound?" I looked out the window. "Who is out there?" I saw nothing.

"¿A quién buscas? Who you looking for?" My mother came out in her robe, drying her hair.

"No one...no one, I thought..." I kept looking out the window.

"That weather is terrible," my mother said, folding the towel and putting it on the dining room chair.

"...I heard a strange sound, like a whale call...a voice, but actually it sounded like...like a woman. But I can't see anything... it's probably nothing."

"You get home late again. Why don't you leave work on time?"

"Well, you know my routine. What else is new?" I went to the refrigerator and got a beer. "My life belongs to my work. My time belongs to everyone else, always the same old bull. But today, I needed a drink, so I went to Joe's tavern."

"You start drinking again?"

"No, mom. I just need to relax... I'm on edge. I used to be like this beer: crisp, refreshing, I had a kick to life...I lost it somehow."

"You sound frustrated, confused. ¿Qué te pasa?"

"¡No sé! I don't know. I don't do anything new; I feel stuck in one place. The same routine every... single... day."

"Así es la vida hijo. We are tired of the same things every day. Society doesn't help; it always wants to entertain us. Why don't you...?"

"Why don't I? WHAT? I work every day, come home, watch T.V., sleep, and work again, the same THING! The weekend comes, rest a little, to start again on Monday. And time goes on, and the years pass by."

"Ay Dios mío." She gets a glass of water.

"Remember that movie where the guy said: *'time is an illusion. It slows down if you look at it; if you ignore it, it flies by.'* it's true. It's been five years since Dad died. It seems like yesterday. Time goes by...I was a kid the other day!"

"Why...why you thinking like that...." My mother looked confused.

"Don't you get it? You save money but then spend it. You buy stuff to put away and store it. You study, thinking you're buying total happiness by getting a piece of paper! That's the ticket to the *American Dream, el sueño americano*. You know...most people that study and graduate are not in the field they studied. NO! Everything is a damn dull routine, and time just keeps going by."

"¿Pero hijo?"

"I'm just saying- is this all life has to offer? It doesn't make any sense; what is the meaning of life if this is it?"

"Ay, your vision is too general," she sighs. "Have you noticed... you've been talking in your sleep?"

"Talking in my sleep?" I laughed. "About what?"

"I don't know. I just know I heard you from my room. It sounded like you said, '*I can't take this anymore. No, no, I need help, I need help.*' I came out immediately, but you were asleep. I don't know for sure. Just the rhythm in your voice scared me. This happened twice last week." The thunder gets louder, and the lightning increases.

"That's crazy. I'm just bored; it makes no sense. I don't talk in my sleep."

"Maybe there's something in the house," she stops and thinks. "I need to do a cleaning."

"Cleaning? What do you mean?"

"I need to clean this house...make our life brighter."
I stared at her.

"Mom...really?"

"Ay, leave me alone. ¿Y tu pintura? Why don't you finish your painting? You have a great talent, but you must give it time and a chance to be great. Find something that gives meaning to your life." I get up and walk to the window and peek out.

"Ma, por favor, a painter must express something about himself in his paintings...when I find that 'something,' I'll finish it, but the way I feel, even the colors bore me."

My sister, Sully, walks in from her bedroom in her pajamas and a notebook.

"Bendición mami."

"Dios te bendiga hija."

"When did you come? I didn't see your car?"

"I got home early, bro. My car is in the shop. My friend dropped me off." She sits on the couch. "Why are you guys talking so loud? There's enough noise with the thunder. I'm trying to write something for my school project, and I can't concentrate."

"What do you have to write?"

"A poem for my English class; I've been dabbling with poetry lately. I've been at it for two days. I can't get an angle."

"Don't you think you're wasting your time, all this studying?" My mother turns and comes right up to my face, pointing.

"Don't you tell her that, don't discourage her. She doing well in going to school; dejala quieta!"

"Take it easy... no es pa' tanto...no big deal, sorry!"

"I never had opportunities you have. I wish I did. I had to take care of my eight brothers and sisters...I know, I know you've heard it before. But it's true. You have opportunities I didn't."

My sister has her own temper; I should know better. She left the big city streets, but the streets never left her. Sully gets up from the couch and walks toward me.

"Oh boy...me *jodi*, I'm screwed!" I whisper, and I move back.

"Hey, I'm making something of myself; don't be trying to drag me down with you. Do you need company in your miseries? Well, it's not with me. You need to start finding something in your life! All you do is complain! But I don't see you doing anything to change it!" She turns, walks to her mother, and hugs her, "Mami, you okay?"

"Sí hija. Moisés, you got to start somewhere. Maybe you should get help, maybe..."

"Oh, go to bed, both of you! Just go to sleep. There's a thunderstorm warning in effect; I heard it on the radio."

Frustrated, I drank my beer and walked to my unfinished painting. Then I hear the sound again. I run to the window.

"Sully! Did you hear that?"

"Hear what?" I open the front door and go outside.

"Hello, anybody out there?" The lightning was rapid; I tried to see where the sound was coming from but couldn't see anything. I go back inside the house.

"Look, you're all soaking wet now. What? You starting to hear things now?" Sully gets the towel from the chair and gives it to me.

"Ay María Santísima!" My mother makes the sign of the cross. "¿Qué te pasa Moisés?"

"Did you hear it? ¿Mami oíste?"

"Yes, I heard it! The thunder, that's all you hear out there!" Sully said.

"No, not the thunder! It's like a...a whale call, I heard it earlier, but now I heard it closer...it sounds like a woman's voice, calling out...singing...a melody."

"Bro, there's no one out there, let alone singing, not with that storm."

I pace back and forth in the living room. "That sound was weird. Maybe it was the wind."

I walk and stand in front of my painting. I looked closely and noticed something strange.

"Did you...do something to this painting...mom?" I look at her.

9

"Yo...no, I don't know how to paint." I look at Sully.

"You're looking at the wrong person when it comes to painting."

"This wasn't here before...I never painted this," I point to the painting of the old house by the shore. Two figures are standing outside the door. "What is going on?"

"Ah...I can't take this. I'm going to sleep, buenas noche. Good night." My mother leaves for her bedroom. Sully gets her notebook and looks at me.

"You know, yesterday, I sat in my room looking out the window, trying to get an idea for this poem. I couldn't help watching the boats on the shore, swaying with the waves, anchored with nowhere to go. . ." She stops and thinks. "Yet, there's a beautiful vast ocean out there to explore. Unless someone got in the boat and took them out to navigate, they would stay there forever, never exploring the world. Um- maybe that's the angle I'm missing." She looks at me. "I'm going to bed too. That thunder is wicked. I hope it doesn't keep me up. Good night."

"Yeah. . . good night." She went to her room; I got another beer.

I go to my painting and look at these two figures. *I don't recall painting this*, I thought. *Maybe I forgot I did.*

I grab a paintbrush from the easel. Holding my beer in one hand, I mimic a painter painting. I was getting drowsy.

I sat on the couch, drinking my beer, then lay down. I began thinking about the day to avoid hearing that strange sound. *What the hell is going on with me? Huh, it's nothing; everybody goes through this,* I thought. Shortly after, I dozed off. I felt a tingling brain vibration...breaking up my thoughts. I had this sensation before, but tonight it was stronger. Then, my muscles tightened. The sound coming from the shore got louder in my head. I was asleep, but my eyes were opened. I was conscious but couldn't move. From my couch, I scan the living room.

Then, I noticed two figures reappearing with every lightning strike. A girl was sitting on the floor wearing a white silk outfit, barefoot, playing with her hair, and a man near the back wall lurking in the shadows; I could not see his face, only his body. My breath caught, and my heart began throbbing. I tried talking but couldn't; I wanted to call my sister but couldn't make a sound. The last thing I remember was hearing static coming from the radio.

Friday Morning

THE WEATHER IS STILL BAD. Lightning followed by thunder.

"Oh my God!" I wake up startled; I look toward the floor and the living room corner. My mother was sweeping.

"Buenos días. Who are you looking for now?"

"I had...the strangest dream last night. I saw a young girl dressed in white and a man over in the dark. It was weird."

"You said, a young girl?" My mother goes to the kitchen and opens a drawer.

"It happened so fast. I dozed off, woke up...couldn't move...and then, there they were."

"Here it is, my dream book." She starts flipping through the pages. "Wait...you saw them here? I thought you said it was a dream?"

"It was a dream...but...I don't know. It seemed so real. I remember trying to call Sully and couldn't speak. I don't remember how I fell asleep."

She's looking through the booklet. "Young girl...it means buena suerte! Good luck. That's good, Moisés."

"Yeah, that's what I need a beautiful young girl to straighten my ass out." I laugh. "Buena suerte, right!"

"I'm going to get you help. I have a friend; she is a spiritualist." She starts looking through her phone book.

"You gotta be kiddin', right? Mom! Don't confuse my life. I don't need more complications. I'll be fine." Sully walks in from her bedroom with her notebook.

"What are you guys talking about now?"

"I had a weird dream last night; two people in our living room, a girl on the floor, and someone over there hiding in the dark."

"And, what's the problem? It's a dream, right? Did they scare you?" Sully asked and sat on the couch.

"They didn't do anything. I can't explain it; they were just there. The girl kept looking at her fingernails and, I think it was a man in the dark...I couldn't see a face. I was, like, paralyzed."

"Why don't you talk about something productive, like real dreams in life, getting a better job, maybe writing a book, finishing *your* painting?"

"Aquí, Doña Josefina, a spiritualist for every occasion." My mother wrote her phone number on a

13

piece of paper and put it on the table. "Here you go." I look at her.

"I don't have time for this; I have to get ready for work." I leave for my room.

"Está bien! If I were you, I would call her today," my mother speaks loud.

"MAMI, WHAT'S WRONG WITH HIM?" Sully asks.

"You know I'm not good with words or advice, but he has reached a point in his life where he's...ay. . . I don't know how to say in English. . . you know, *'ha llegado a una calle sin salida.'*"

"Oh, he's at a dead-end street?"

"Sí, sí! You know, you there, and you have no place to go ahead. You need to come out, start again, and find another way. You see what I mean, entiendes?"

Sully gets up from the couch and goes to the painting. "I see life as a journey. The journey is fun when you know where you're going. Traveling in circles with no destination is hard, like a ship captain without a compass." Sully walks to her mother.

"I know...I've seen so many people in my lifetime who have lost their way...they regret their lives. I worry about him. Shh...he's coming."

"See you tonight," I grab my umbrella and leave for work.

"He'll be okay; he's just going through something," Sully says, putting her arm around her.

"Yo sé hija, I know. Gracias. It's just a mother worrying about her grown-up son."

"Okay, I have to finish my poem; it's due on Monday." Sully kisses her on the forehead.

Friday Evening

I GET HOME FROM WORK WITH A SIX-PACK. Sully is at the dining table putting away her school stuff.

"Hi, Sully."

"Hi, brother."

"How's that poem going?"

"I finally got an idea, an angle...thanks to you."

"Thanks to me? Don't tell me...I inspired a poem?"

"You sure did. All this talk about boredom, routine, and this weather."

"Wow, can I hear it?"

"It's not ready yet...by the weekend. I'll let you know. Bye, need to do some research."

"Hey." She turns around. "Sorry about yesterday, it wasn't right what I said...you know...about school. Keep it up; you're on the right track."

"We're good." She goes to her room.

"Yeah...I've been on the wrong track." I get a beer. My mother walks in, rubbing her neck. Then I smelled *Vicks* making its way to my nose.

"Drinking again? Keep it up; you're con-tri-bu-ting to your nightmares or whatever you saw...how was your day?"

"How was my day? You know, mom, you should be in a comedy club; how was my day? Like always, same thing, nothing new. No, wait, wait. I had a Cuban sandwich. Yeah...roasted pork, ham, cheese, pickles, and a little spread of mustard. I had forgotten how good they were. That's the newest thing I've done, other than the sammmmmme old thing."

"I see things haven't changed."

"I feel worse today. I had that damn dream in my head all day. You know, I think I'm going coo-coo." She walks to the table, picks up the paper, and hands it to me.

"You're not going crazy; you need direction. Here's Doña Josefina's number. Maybe she can tell you something."

"What can she tell me, mom? No, I don't want my head full of scenarios, schemes of who's doing what to me!"

"You want some Vicks?"

"Vicks? I don't have a headache."

"Vicks cures everything- might clear your head." She rubs some on her nose. "I go to bed now; I'm tired, working in the house all day. Don't think too much, ten fé; have faith that things will change for the better. Buenas noches, hijo."

"Good night, mom."

I SIT ON THE COUCH, DRINKING MY BEER and looking at the piece of paper.

"Doña Josefina, yeah right. I don't need some spiritualist complicating my life." I crumble it and throw it back on the table.

Thunder still lurks in the background; lightning is sporadic. I start thinking of my youth; I remember the good old days. Life was simpler. Play stickball, baseball, and punchball. Not a worry in the world.

I take a sip of my beer. I start to doze off, then a loud rumble of thunder; I drop my beer. I open my eyes and notice a fog entering the living room. Then I hear it again, that mystical voice. I get up and run to the window, trying to look through the rain. I see nothing. I hear static coming from the radio, though it is off. *What's going on?*

"Looking for something?" I turn, and the girl is sitting on the floor, dressed like a ballerina, all in white. She's barefoot and beautiful. I look toward the back wall, and the figure is in the dark.

"Not you again. Who are you?" I run to check the front door; I look in my mother's bedroom; she is sleeping. I walk to Sully's room, and she is sleeping. "How did you get in here? What do you want?"

"You called," a man's voice comes from the shadow.

"I called? What's going on, two nights in a row?" The girl gazes at her fingernails.

"We heard you in your sleep, murmuring." She imitates me, groaning. "*I can't take this anymore. No, no, I need help; I need help.*"

"I have not called anyone! How did you get into my house?" I look at her. "Excuse me! What are you doing in my living room? You just come in whenever you want? Who are you?"

She passes her fingers through her hair.

"We're here because of you. You need help." She looks down. "But I can't help you right now." She points to her ankles. "You see, I'm not free to help you."

I start laughing- I couldn't help it. "What else could happen to me? I am losing it; am I going crazy?" I start pacing the living room. "I got to get this damn dream out of my head."

"Maybe it's not a dream," the girl said, looking up at me from the floor.

"That's it! It's stress. It's making me see things. You're not really here. You're just a fabrication of what I'm going through, my imagination playing tricks on me."

"Come on, that's cliché-ish." I walk up to her to see if she looks fuzzy, like a dream. She grabs my hand. I panic, trying to let go, but I can't. She makes me feel her hair.

"Is it real? Is it a fabrication of your imagination?" I pull back and walk away, trying to make sense of what is happening. I can't tell if I'm dreaming or awake.

"Oh wait! Is this about money?" The girl stops playing with her hair and looks at me from the floor.

"Money? You are so out of touch."

"You're speaking in puzzles, young lady. Out of touch?" I walk to the window. "Okay, I was thinking about my childhood, dozed off, the thunder woke me up, and I heard that strange mystical voice."

"There you go again, mumbling under your breath, *and thunder woke me up,*" she makes fun of me.

"Then, I turn around, and you are here! AGAIN! Where the hell did you come from?"

"You'll find out, all in good time," she said.

"No! I need to know now! Where did you come from? Both of you!"

"You called!"

"Oh, that was really cute; you both answered at the same time."

The girl gets up from the floor. I move back, but she is inhibited from going far because of the chains around her ankles.

"Don't you recognize who I am? No, me conoces?" She asks me.

"You speak Spanish? Damn, I've never had a bilingual dream. Now, I know I'm losing it." I walked up to her and stared at her. She tilts her face from side to side.

"No...don't recognize you. We've never met."

"I knew it... it's hard to look inward and meet your essence."

"Look inward? What in the world are you talking about?" She combs her hair. "Man, this is not making any sense. Alright, alright. I admit it; my mother was right; maybe I've had too much to drink. I'm just going to sleep it off." I walk to the couch and lie down. "You are not here, and you hiding in the dark. Don't you have anything to say? I'm not giving in to this bullshit. You'll be gone by the morning." I lay down, looking at her. "Aren't you cold with that little bitty dancing outfit on, and what's with the chains around your ankles?"

She ignores me, waving her hands up in the air like a ballerina. I close my eyes. I want to sleep and wake up normal, but she starts talking.

"Dreams are part of our subconscious state of mind, where anxieties are stored and released, sometimes in nightmares." I open my eyes. "They try to relate a message to our conscious state of mind," she continues, still waving her hands.

"Now you're into some philosophical shit. This is not real. You're just a dream. You're not here; you are nothing but an image."

I try to sleep but can't. She goes back to sit on the floor and plays with her dress.

I observe her and think to myself, she looks real. This can't be a nightmare. I'm not even scared. Nightmares are supposed to be scary, spooky, dark, and certainly don't have beautiful girls in them.

"Are you ready to listen to us, so we can try to help you?" The girl asks.

"Listen to what? You're in my head; how could you possibly help me, and how do you know I need help?" She stops waving her arms and looks at me.

"This is serious, Moisés. You could think and make up all the excuses, try to reason, but let me be clear, you only get this opportunity once in your life. Very rarely does it come back for a second chance."

"Wait a minute! How do you know my name?" I jump off the couch. "Oh shit, now I get it! You're Doña Josefina's friends; did she send you guys?" She gets up from the floor and walks toward me.

"Stop it! Stop blaming your boredom, routine, the beer, Doña Josefina...and take responsibility for your life!" She walks away. "So, let me know, MOISES, when you're ready. I could be helping someone else who really wants it."

A voice comes out of the shadow. "I can't help you; the only thing I can do is be here. It's not my time yet." Frustrated with this dream-nightmare, I get a beer, walk, and stand in front of the shadow area.

"Wow, you finally said something...it's not my time yet?" I start laughing. "You're useless! Great explanation! You're the nightmare, not her!" The man steps forward but is still in the shadow.

"I wouldn't say that; I could be a continuous nightmare for the rest of your life."

"So, if you can't help me, there in the shadow and you all shackled up. What are you both doing here?"

"You called!" They both say together again. I laugh like a mad scientist and drink my beer.

"Wow, in harmony. What? You guys rehearse this stuff? Okay, let's say you are here to help me since you both made it your business to barge in once again. I need an explanation...tonight!" She walks closer to me.

"Moisés, wake up and smell the coffee! Oh wow! *Wake up and smell the coffee*; get it, *wake up!* She laughs.

"I'm glad you find my situation amusing."

"It's very simple; I know everyone and everything." She walks, dragging her chain around the living room.

"What kind of nonsense are you saying? So, you know everyone and everything? This is becoming a comedy, another element I never heard of; a funny nightmare." Then she starts dancing, but her anchors hurt her ankles, so she stops.

"I'm ambition, imagination, happiness, the essence of life. But most people ignore me. Those who know me and work hard reach their highest potential in life, but most people don't bother." She tries to dance again but is restricted by the chains. I listen and drink my beer. Then I walk to the man.

"Okay, she's explained her purpose; I don't understand, but at least she's trying. What's your angle? There in the shadows of darkness."

"I have no purpose," he said.

"I thought so...do I know you? You sound familiar. What's your name?" There is no answer.

"Okay, how about shadow man? That fits you." She interrupts.

"I reside in all humans: in you, in children, in prostitutes, men in jail, in the homeless, in the rich and the poor, in the elderly, your beautiful poetic sister, and your lovely mother." She looks over my shoulders and embraces herself, her face pondering in love. I turn and see my mother come out of her bedroom.

"Mom?" She doesn't hear me. She gets a glass of water, walks to the couch, and looks down like she's looking at me.

"Mom?" I call her again, but no response. She walks back to her room. I look at the girl.

"You leave her and my sister out of this. They're not part of this nightmare."

"She's worried about you."

"This is so frustrating. Why can't I wake up from this mess?"

"I live in you, Moisés."

"You live in me? Yeah, in my head!"

"I know your insecurity, your anxieties, your pain, your lack of self-love, your daily routine is eating you up, and you're living a damn boring life." Her voice was getting stern. "I know everything, even the color of your underwear." She says sarcastically.

"Oh, I'm taking full advantage of this therapy session. Okay, I'm not going to deny it...that I am feeling bored. But how do you know all this about me? Are you trying to tell me something through this nightmare?"

"So, you still think this is a nightmare? You see, Moisés, man insists on paying more attention to his external world, being entertained, and ignoring the core of his inner being."

"Can you get to the point?" I get another beer.

"BOREDOM is the lack of stimulation, which leads to empty feelings; when repeated, it leads to ROUTINE, which leads to this..." she points at me. "...a beautiful life becomes dull. Man's external life will not fulfill his emptiness. The treasure is internal. Where goals live, the purpose of life! Passion!"

"Young lady, everybody is too busy to think about the inner self, stimulation- treasures! Just tell me, what do I need to do?"

"Hold on, hold on," she laughs. "I have another one. Check this out. Maybe I'm your *wake-up call!*" She laughs hysterically. "Get it? 'Wake-up call.' Oh my, I haven't laughed like this in years."

"I'm glad you're finding humor...how long is this shit; nightmares don't last this long. I should have woken up by now."

"I'm sorry, Moisés, but sometimes you need a good laugh." She walks to me, serious. "You still don't know who I am?" I look at her, trying to recognize her. She sat back on the floor and rubbed her ankle.

"I've never seen you in my life."

"Yeah, I'm not surprised. Society offers many distractions, and most people buy into it. But, when they face a couple of obstacles, they settle for less. In their silence, they lack that inner strength...they give up and throw in the towel. *I'm done! Finire! Fertig! Tapusin! Terminer! No mas!* Some realize it, but time is running out for those who don't."

"Let me help you take those chains off."

"Do not touch me! You cannot remove these chains; they don't require a key."

"What do you mean?" I move back.

"What does she mean?" I ask the shadow man- he doesn't answer. Silence occupies the darkness. "You know, shadow man, your presence here bothers me. You are taking up space; if you have no purpose here, go, leave! What? Do you have a scar? Are you blind? Don't worry; nobody will see you, always hiding in your precious shadow," I walk closer, "...what's with the compass?" Silence. I walk away. Then a voice breaks through the darkness.

26

"I live in the shadow...you've...created."

"Me? Oh, now it's me?" I started laughing.

"A hopeless shadow, unsure. I don't want to be here, but you called."

"Oh...keep going; this is the longest you've spoken. I'm listening."

"It's too soon."

"Are you hearing yourself? It's too soon for what? Buddy, you know you're more confused than me. Leave! You're useless!"

"You don't understand!" The shadow man's voice gets louder.

"What don't I understand? Please explain." The girl looks up and shouts.

"Don't show him!" I turn to look at her.

"Don't show me? Don't show me what?"

"He needs to know!" The shadow man screams at the girl.

"Don't show him! Don't you see, it could jeopardize his future." I was desperate to get answers.

"I don't care, tell me! I need an answer!" The shadow man steps up but is still in the dark. The girl gets up and drags herself toward the shadow man. She stands between us.

"Don't show him; he needs to discover it for himself; we haven't given him enough time."

"He must know! He has to face his dilemma! It could save his future!" The girl starts to weep.

"Don't show him, please. Give me more time; he's not ready." The thunder gets louder. "I've seen this before; he must realize it himself." Lightning flashes through the window. "He needs to recognize us; that way, he'll understand why we're here."

I can't see the shadow man's face. I look at her, and she's not moving, standing still, looking at the shadow area, shaking her head, "no, no, please," she repeats in a low voice.

Then I see the shadow man slowly leaving the comfort of his darkness.

"Okay, now we're getting somewhere. Come on; you're doing great. Come on, a little more." The house lights dim against the occasional lightning. The shadow man finally leaves the dark behind and steps into the light.

"What?... What the hell is this? Oh, my God, who are you? No, no, I have to wake up. This has finally turned into a horrible nightmare. What's going on? Why can't I move?" The shadow man walks up to my face.

"Go away, leave me alone. Go back to your shadow!" I break loose from my trance and run to the couch. I lay down and tried to wake up from the nightmare. I put the couch pillow over my head.

"Moisés, wake up!" I scream, "wake up!"

SATURDAY EVENING

"BUT MAMI, I'M SORRY he has to do something; he's always complaining."

"Shhh! You wake up, Moisés. Yo se hija, I know. I just don't know what else to tell him. I not up-to-date on things...with my eighth-grade education."

"Mami, stop talking like that; it has nothing to do with school. Your life and experience are valuable educators."

"I don't know, with all this new... *technologia*. On the Spanish channel the other day, I heard about this new thing called...um, how do they call it? Hay como se llama? *Yohuhu, yowho*, it sounds like the chocolate drink."

"Chocolate drink? Yoohoo?"

"Sí, sí ese. That's it."

"You mean Yahoo....yeah, it's new on the internet." Sully laughs.

"Shhh, stop it."

"I can't help it; you make me laugh."

"Ay, que se levante!" They both laugh.

"Anyway, you gave me this new shampoo bottle about two weeks ago...remember?"

"Yeah, I remember; how was it?"

"It's okay, but something happened to me while washing my hair."

"Que paso? You slip? You fell?"

"No, mom, I read the words they put on the bottom...it made me think."

"What do you mean?"

"Remember I screamed out from the bathroom and asked you a question?"

"Hay hija, I don't remember. Your mother's memory is going."

"Anyway, I wrote a poem; can I read it to you?"

"¡Si! Go ahead."

"It needs a little work, but here it goes. It's called,

For Dry and Damaged Hair

Showering, I took the bottle of shampoo.
Read the label to make sure it wasn't

                   the conditioner.

Poured the shampoo,
rubbed it deep into my scalp,
soapsuds covered me like gravy.
With one eye open, I read the label:

               for Dry and Damaged Hair.

I wondered.

I kept rubbing, scrubbing, and massaging. It felt straight, long, zesty, you know...like the commercials.

On my second wash, I reread the label, but this time, like a question,
> *for Dry and Damaged Hair?*

My thoughts ricochet like a marble in a pinball machine.

I rinsed it out, got out of the shower, combing my hair, I heard my mind questioning my ego,
> *for Dry and Damaged Hair?*

"Yo, Mami, do you think I have dry and damaged hair?"

"No, hija, there no such thing as damaged hair."

"Bravo! Bravo hija! I love it!"
"Shhh."
"Ay, que se joda, wakey up!" Sully puts her hand over her mother's mouth.

"Mami, do you remember when you told me? *There's no such thing as damaged hair.*"
"Yes, I remember now."

"You have no idea how profound your answer was. I mean...who has the right to determine who has good hair, bad hair, or, let alone, damaged hair? And then put it on a shampoo bottle! I feel that sometimes we are conditioned. I wondered how many of us live our lives with one eye closed."

"You're right, and people settle. They give up searching for the truth. That's what's happening to...." She buckles her lips toward Moisés. "He needs to fucis!"

"He needs to what? Sully laughs. "What are you trying to say?"

"You know, enfocar!" She points to her eyes. "You know, fuc...is!"

Sully laughs. Moisés opens his eyes slightly and moves around on the couch. "You mean focus. Say focus..."

"Fuc...is!" Sully laughs, covering her mouth.

"Forget it, mom."

"Don't make fun of my English," she fixes her hair rollers.

Sully looks at her watch. "Oh my God, I have to get back to writing. Let me eat something first." She gets a bowl of Cheerios.

"Hijo despierta, wakey up. You've been sleeping all day." She gets the broom and makes believe she's going to hit Moisés and giggles.

"Man, I wish I could sleep like that; yo' bro wake up!"

"What?" I wake up dazed.

"¿Qué paso, another nightmare?" Sully asks.

"You want to tell me where these markings and scratches came from?" My mother asks, pointing to the floor.

"Markings?" I look at the floor. "Scratches?"

"Did you go outside again last night? The floor was wet this morning."

"Floor wet? La muchacha, the girl!" I start remembering.

"What? You're having wet dreams now?" Sully laughs, eating her Cheerios.

"I have a headache. I had the same dream...but it turned into a horrible nightmare last night." It takes me a while to get up and sit on the couch. "The girl had these small anchors chained to her ankle. You know, like the boats have." I get up and walk to the shadow area. "The man behind the shadow finally came out, but he had no...facial features, only a mouth. He had an entire body but no face. Last night was definitely a nightmare."

"He had no face? Only a mouth? Hui, scary," Sully said.

"Keep watching those horror movies," my mother said, making the sign of the cross.

"The girl talked about my insecurities, the reason for my boredom; she spoke about men buying into the routine of life."

"And being *conditioned*," Sully emphasized.

"She spoke in general; she knew about my problem. But, when he came out, the shadow man didn't have a face. I don't understand. Why would I dream something like that?"

"Did you call Doña Josefina?" Mom asked sarcastically. Sully looked at her.

"Doña Josefina? I heard you mentioned her name yesterday. Is she the lady who said I was on drugs and hanging with the wrong people, and we find out later that her son was the one that got busted? Yeah, she's a spiritualist alright." She puts her bowl on the counter.

"It seemed like they were trying to help me. I was never a believer in all this *dream symbolism* stuff. But it seemed so real."

"I'm going to bed; my back hurts," Mom said, yawning.

"So early?"

"So early? Son las nueve...it's nine o'clock at night."

"Nine o'clock?!"

"You slept all day. I let you sleep because it's Saturday." She folds her apron. "Sully and I cleaned a little. Then we sat talking all this time, laughing, and you didn't hear anything. Good night hope you don't have a nightmare again; it's scary, que miedo." She goes to her room.

"Wow! That was some nightmare. Aren't you scared to go back to sleep?" Sully asks.

"You know, I'm not. I want to meet with them again. Find out why the shadow man is faceless. I hope they show up tonight. You think dreams try to tell us something, Sully?"

"I think so."

"This feels so real. I don't know whether this is a nightmare or real."

"Oh well. I'm done with my poem. I'll read it to you tomorrow. Good night."

"Great, I can't wait to hear it. I'm going to lie down again to see if they come back."

I GO TO THE COUCH, LIE DOWN, AND TRY TO SLEEP. Thunder lingers in the distance. I feel electrical pulses bouncing in my head, interfering with my thoughts. Suddenly, I opened my eyes and found myself looking in the refrigerator for something to eat. I get a cup of rice pudding and sit on the couch. I looked around the living room, waiting. A mist forms. Then, I faintly hear the mystical voice mixed with the thunder. I get up and walk to the window, look but I don't see anyone.

"You still don't know who I am?" The girl said from behind me. I turn, and she's sitting on the floor, playing with her hair.

"How did I get from the couch to the window...I turned around, and you're in my living room? No sort of transition. I mean, I'm not upset. I'm glad you're back. Now...why doesn't he have a face?"

"Because you have not given me a face!" said the shadow man.

"Me? Okay, I know this is a nightmare, and you fit right in, but I don't understand. I haven't given you a face?"

"Have you ever had a dream and said, '*it felt so real?*'" She said, getting up from the floor.

"Yes! This one!"

"Right! This is one of them. Moisés, we are you! I am your soul; he is your future!" The shadow man steps out of the darkness.

"I'm your tomorrow! The outcome of the consequences of your life. Right now, I'm a deformed future if you don't do something soon."

"No, it can't be, you cannot be my future, it's not true, don't play with me! Besides, these things don't happen in real life. A man with no face?"

The girl interjects, "This is precisely why we're here, because, in real life, it happens. People walk around lost all the time. If you don't identify a purpose, your future is deformed."

I laugh. "But you're not real, honey. You're a dream. I mean...you don't look like a nightmare- but he does!"

"Moisés, choose your words carefully; he is you, and your life is not a nightmare." She said.

"I don't understand how you...him...could be me! What kind of game is this?"

"This inner battle happens to people every day. They question, who am I? They struggle to find something meaningful in their lives...they're unclear about their future."

"Yeah, but it doesn't show up like this...like him." I pace the living room. A sadness comes over me; I feel dizzy. I sit on the couch. "I thought you came to help me. You just added more anxiety to my life!" She walks up to me.

"You only see the outside world, but never look inward where your purpose is; where your happiness lives...hidden...for you to discover." I get up and walk away from them. I look at them from a distance.

"Don't reject me." The shadow man speaks. "It'll get worst as you get older...if you don't address it now." The girl stands by the shadow man.

"I see you constantly pacing back and forth, looking for me, your soul, your inner self. So, here I am."

I keep staring at them, trying to make sense, wondering if I should try to get up.

"We live in everyone, but we can't help you unless you want to find a definition, a meaning to your life. But we're here to help you if you wish."

I walk up to her. We both stare at each other.

"So, you've come to show me the outcome; if I don't give my life a definition, a meaning, a purpose, this is what's to be expected of my future?" I look over at the shadow man.

The shadow man steps back into the shadow. His voice pierces through the darkness.

"I came out too soon. I'm sorry. I didn't want to shock you. But you couldn't see it in your conscience state of mind, so I came to show you." I walk up to him.

"Well, couldn't you find a better way to make your point? You come sneaking in every night and then show me this."

The girl starts dancing, waving her hands. "There are too many distractions in our society. People don't think of their future. They walk blindly without a spirit, just a body of flesh and blood with no meaning. The routine eats their time slowly. Regrets creep in for not doing something significant with their life." She mimics a person complaining. *'I should have done this when I was younger.'* They reach a faceless future living in a dark inner shadow without noticing. I see it all the time. Then the infamous phrase, *'It's not my fault,'* they start blaming others."

"You're telling me I have no vision?" They stay silent. "Say something!" She whispers to me.

"It's a noisy world out there. So many opinions and views. Silence is good. But it makes people uncomfortable...they don't want to hear my inner voice." She plays with her long hair. I walk to the mirror in the living room and look at myself.

"Your eyes are empty; your soul is void of meaning. You will never see your deformed face. Your deformity is inside. Many camouflage themselves, making others think they're okay."

"I can't accept this. I feel my life means more than this; I mean...I was going through a rough time. Well, you know...boredom...tired of my routine."

"Rough time?" She chuckles. "Let me tell you what a rough time is if you keep at this pace." I turn and face her. She comes and walks in circles around me. "You are still young, Moisés. The road ahead of you is long. Here comes the rough part. As you get older, the road ahead of you becomes shorter. If you do nothing with your life, you naturally start looking back at the road you left behind. You see at a distance the opportunities you've allowed to pass by. The book you were supposed to write! The song you were supposed to sing! The time wasted on insignificant things! The rest of the road ahead could be full of regrets!"

I walk back to the mirror. "My father always told me, 'Don't leave for tomorrow what you could do today, for that tomorrow may never come.' Now I understand."

The shadow man steps into the light. "He was right. But don't give up, don't sell yourself to conformity. I'm your premature future, but it doesn't have to be this way. You must confront me. Only you can change this." He points to his faceless face. I walk and stand in front of him.

39

"I can't believe I'm standing in front of my future. You're... like a forecast of my life."

"You still have plenty of time," the girl said, "Man is much bigger, *mas gránde* than they think. That is why I've been responding to your anxiety." She sings in the strange mystical voice I kept hearing. I turned around and looked at her.

"It was you all this time. You were the call?" She nods and starts to dance again, smiling.

"Many ignore me. I try to show up in different ways. Sometimes I'll make you notice a beautiful sunset to give you enthusiasm. Other times I might let you meet someone successful." She mimics a businessperson, "'*It's a pleasure to meet you, sir,*'" to make you aware of your own potential. As I said, many ignore me, escape...they don't allow me to show them and enrich their lives." She sits on the floor. "Some say. . . '*It's too hard; I don't have the time.*' But they always make time for the things they want to do! Am I right?" I fall to my knees. I feel a pain in the gut of my stomach.

"I have no vision? My future is deformed!" I look and notice her making the same physical gestures as if she's feeling my pain.

Then she gets up from the floor. The shadow man steps back into the dark. She speaks into the air as she dances.

"Those who are set in their ways get lost in the turmoils of life. In the storm, they navigate without a compass. There is no connection with me or their true essence. Everything is ego: me, me, me!" Her voice gets stern. "Look at society: the crimes, men killing each other, drugs, wars for religious rights and political views, racism, innocent lives lost, children suffering at the hands of grown-ups. They only listen to their ego and selfishness, color-blind to skin color. But I always give an opportunity for change, for hope." She sits back on the floor and starts combing her hair.

I walk around mystified, questions bouncing in my head, thinking...I cannot allow my life to end like this. No, no... I walk up to my painting and realize...this is what I've always wanted to do, be a painter and express my inner world on canvas. This is it!

"Moisés, when you find your passion..." she looks at the painting, "you will wake up every morning eager to strive toward your dream. The routine turns into discipline. I've seen it; those who work with me go far. Those that walk with me have reached unimaginable wisdom and knowledge." I hear a voice coming from the shadow.

"It's not that hard; there is no word in the dictionary that doesn't have a meaning...life needs a meaning. The more you identify with your purpose, the more you and I are one, and your future will have beautiful features." Then I look down at the girl.

"Your chains? Where are your chains?" She's asleep. I sit next to her on the floor.

"You look so pure, untouched by the philosophies, political views, and fanatical religious doctrines. Unaffected by the rust built upon our souls from constant disappointments and hurts. You are free from parasites attached to us that govern our decisions, misguide our direction...suffocate our essential self. You are untainted, waiting for us to make something useful with our lives."

The voice comes from the shadow again. "Man camouflages their true sense of self with patched-up personalities and shallow ideologies. Self-love is vital. That's where the truth lives." The girl wakes up. She stares at me and smiles. She gets up and dances freely, unrestrained by chains.

"Those who have kept me close have defined their purpose and lived productive lives amidst their daily challenges. While others have become great leaders in the world: *Abraham Lincoln, Mahatma Gandhi, Martin Luther King Jr., Madre Teresa of Calcutta, Rosa Parks, Roberto Clemente, Cesar Chávez, Nelson Mandela, my dear Albert Einstein, Lady Diana,* and many more. They defined their lives and then gave to the world; some even changed the course of history."

She points to her ankles while still dancing. "You see, Moisés, I feel free; I no longer have those heavy, uncomfortable anchors dragging me down. It means you're changing internally. You're connecting with ME!

Just know, don't let boredom settle in like barnacles on a sunken ship."

Then, I hear a violin playing. I look around but see no one.

"Oh, nobody is playing. It's the sound of life, rejoicing a positive change."

"Would you care to dance?" the girl asks me.

"I would...love to." I grab her hand and dance.

"You have freed me...US! We can go toward your future together, discovering more great things about you." I look toward the shadow man, and I'm surprised.

"Why do I see his nose?" I ask the girl.

"The more you connect with your inner self, *THAT'S ME!* the more your future begins to clear. Just...the mere fact that you are seriously thinking about it, your future starts to take form. You're seeing it yourself; do I need to say any more?"

I look again, and the shadow man steps back in the dark. I walk over, and he is no longer there.

"He's gone," I look at the girl.

"You'll see him...*YOURSELF* again in the future." I turn, and the girl stretches her hand out to me. She grabs them, and we lie on the couch together. As I fall asleep, I hear the violin fade into the distance.

SUNDAY MORNING

"GOOD SUNDAY MORNING. The sun is finally out, the birds are chirping, and the storm is behind us!" The radio announcer said the forecast as I walked into the house.

"Ma?" I lower the radio. "Mom? Come here!" I take out the groceries.

"Ya voy! Be right there!" She screams from her bedroom. Then she comes into the kitchen.

"Mom, today begins a new day."

"Flowers for me, gracias hijo! Thank you so much. Oh, you went shopping, I see." She gets a vase for her flowers.

"I got us some breakfast. Where is Sully? I also got this." I take out a complete set of brushes and paint for my drawing. She puts the flowers in a vase.

"That's wonderful. What happened? Was it last night?" She looks at me, waiting for an answer. Sully comes in, holding her notebook.

"What's going on? Oh, you got breakfast; someone is feeling better, I see." I grab Sully and lift her in the air.

"Yeah, Sully, today is a new day. No more boring routine, no more feeling like, *you know what.*"

"Oh my God, I'm so excited for you. It's always so good when that fog clears up, and you begin to see clearly. Hold on; I got something for you." She reaches into her school bag, takes out a box, and gives it to me.

"For me?" I opened it, and it was a compass. I look at her, surprised; I remember seeing this before. I walk to the shadow man area holding the compass in my hand.

"What's wrong? Don't you like it?" Sully asks, curious.

"Yes...yes! I remembered something...I love it."

"Sorry I didn't wrap it."

"A compass...nice! Thank you!"

"Just a reminder that life is a journey. It was the only way to navigate and not get lost in the old days. Imagine a ship in a storm, navigating without a compass. So, look at your compass whenever you feel lost and find a way to get back on course."

"Sully, this is perfect, thank you." We hug. Mother sets the table.

"So, are you going to tell us what happened?" Mom asks.

"I'll tell you as we eat, I'm hungry."

"Wait, wait. I want to read my poem," Sully takes out her notes. "Mami, sit. I hope you don't get angry, but I took your situation and everything going on, got inspired, and wrote this poem."

"Sully, I'm glad I inspired you. Go right ahead; I can't wait to hear it." She holds her hand-written sheet.

"Okay, here it goes." She takes a deep breath and reads off the paper.

Anchored Soul

You're anchored
on the old dock,
like an old boat
for some years now,
day into night
night into morning.

Rusted from inactivity,
barnacles live rent-free.

Same view, nothing new.
Waves invite you to venture
into the vast ocean,
into uncharted waters,
into unpredictable weather,
and leave behind boredom.

Like a chained prisoner,
your anchor rests below.
You fear the unexpected,

it covers you like algae.

Don't drown!
Throw boredom overboard.
Don't join other wrecks below.

Pull up your anchor
and sail toward a new horizon!

Mom and I give her a standing ovation—Sully bows.

"Fantastico, Sully! That was great! You captured *exactly* what I was going through!"

"Bravo hija, Bravo. I'm so proud of you!" Mom runs and hugs Sully.

"I like writing poems. I'm changing my major to writing."

"Okay, let's eat; I want to tell you what happened last night."

The Present

My sister Sully read that poem that Sunday morning 30 years ago. She went on to become a nationally recognized Latina Poet, well respected in the literary community.

I haven't stopped thinking about that evening. I don't know if that experience was a dream or reality, but it was real to me. It all seemed to fit perfectly; the weather reflected how I felt. The strange sound was like an S.O.S. signaling for help. I felt much better after those three days; it changed my life forever. I guess the moral of my experience is that you must find a dream, a purpose, something to strive for, and make it a passion that will drive you toward succeeding in what you want. Those who choose to settle for less or have it easy will have a deformed future without meaning unless they decide to change.

Today, I'm a painter. Since that weekend, I've traveled the world exhibiting my work. My last exhibit was at the Guggenheim Arts Gallery in New York City. And yes, I finally finished the painting I started, and Mami, may she rest in peace, kept nagging me to finish. It became one of my signature paintings, winning numerous art awards. I named it...Forecast-Pronóstico.

About the Author

VICTOR VELEZ was born in Puerto Rico but raised in New York City; he started writing in the early 80s as a freelance writer for the newspaper, *"El Nuevo Amanecer."* He studied Communication Arts at St. Francis College in Brooklyn, New York. He is a movie lover, a photographer, and an active Salsa and Latin Jazz musician. Author of sixteen books, he teaches at the Clifton Cultural Arts Center in Cincinnati, Ohio, where he currently lives.

ALSO BY VICTOR VELEZ
A Quest for Answers: A Personal Journey
Conga Blues
Salsa on the Square: A Summer of Photos
¿Dónde Estás, Señor?
Images: Thirty Years of Photography
Divine Reflections
Wandering Soul
Salsa in the 'Nati
The Triduum of All Hallows
You Live Inside!

Made in the USA
Columbia, SC
09 September 2024

41471504R00036